The Giant and the Frippit

Linda Strachan
Illustrated by James Cotton

RIGBY

At the top of a tree
lived a small, brown frippit.
At the bottom of the tree
lived a giant.

2

The giant was a kind giant.

He liked all the animals in the wood.

All the animals liked him.

One day, the giant invited everyone to a picnic.
The frippit didn't want to go and
he didn't want the giant to have a picnic.

So, when the giant was playing with the animals, the frippit ran down the tree and took the giant's picnic.

The giant looked for his picnic,
but he couldn't find it.

The giant knocked at the frippit's door.

KNOCK! KNOCK!

"Have you got my picnic?" asked the giant.

"No, I don't have it," said the frippit.

BUT HE DID!

One night, the giant was reading
a bedtime story.

"Shhh!" said the frippit.

"Stop reading that story! I can't sleep!"

The next day, when the giant was chopping
some wood, the frippit ran down
the tree and took the giant's book.

The giant looked for his book,
but he couldn't find it.

The giant knocked at the frippit's door.

KNOCK! KNOCK!

"Have you got my book?" asked the giant.

"No, I don't have it," said the frippit.

BUT HE DID!

That night the wind blew and blew.
The wind shook the tree and
the frippit fell out of his house.

He fell
all the way
down
to the foot
of
the
tree.

"**Help!**" he cried.

13

The giant saw the frippit falling.
He put out his hand, and
the frippit fell into it.

The giant took the frippit into his house and gave him some food.

Then the giant put the frippit to bed and read him a story.

"I'm sorry I took your book," said the frippit.

"And I'm sorry I took your picnic.

I'll never do that again."

From that day on,
the giant and the frippit
were good friends.